Far Walker

OTHER YEARLING BOOKS YOU WILL ENJOY:

Illustrations by
Susan Gustavson

Far Walker

by Larry Leonard

A Yearling Book

Published by
Dell Publishing
a division of
Bantam Doubleday Dell Publishing Group, Inc.
666 Fifth Avenue
New York, New York 10103

ISBN: 0-440-40478-9

Reprinted by arrangement with Breitenbush Publications

Printed in the United States of America

August 1991

10 9 8 7 6 5 4 3 2 1
CWO

This one's for Helen Agness Nyhus

Far Walker

One

His name was David, and even the day he was born he struck the other lemmings as most unusual. For one thing, he didn't cry out and scramble for the furry warmth of his mother as did his six brothers and sisters. David just sat there, his face screwed up into an old man's grimace, trying to look around in a dark burrow with eyes that were not all that good yet.

It is usually several days before a lemming will open his eyes, let alone actually attempt to see. But not David. He was ready to get at the business of living, first thing.

Within hours of his birthing, he had bumped into everything around his mother, causing her great consternation. It bothered his father, too, this unusual behavior.

"It's nothing, dear. Just a phase," he said.

Still, David's mother fretted. Unusual behavior was considered a very dangerous thing among lemmings. Many felt one such as David could even bring on the *madness*.

As David quickly grew stronger — much faster than his siblings because he was the most active — he explored the burrow from its darkest recesses to the very mouth where his father stood constant guard. His first curiosities were about that place. He wondered why it was dark part of the time there, and why it was light part of the time. More than anything he wanted to see what was out there.

"In due time," his father would say, settling his great six-inch bulk in the doorway. "In due time."

David would have to be satisfied with nothing more than a crack of light and his imagination.

Then one day David discovered something. He was scratching at a shadowed pebble in the deepest part of the burrow and getting quite frustrated because it wouldn't budge any more than his father. He took to scraping the dirt below it and clunk! It fell right out on the floor. Where the pebble had been was a hole bigger than David's mouse-sized head.

Well now, he thought. I wondered what these claws on my feet were for. Now I know. Then another thought struck him. That's how the burrow had happened. It had been dug! And what had been dug this far could be dug farther. He would see that light for himself! He set to work happily, scratching at the back of the pebble hole.

His progress was swift because the ground was soft. In no time at all there was nothing showing but his short stub of a tail and a steady stream of dirt. But, regardless of what strange gifts he had been born with, David lacked something all lemmings have naturally: a sense of direction underground. Instead of burrowing upwards, he went sideways. In a very short time he fell right through the wall of the next lemming house. Worse yet, he landed right on top of a big father lemming. And worst of all, this particular father lemming was the clan chief lemming. A fellow who did not like either unusual behavior *or* surprises.

"Yipe!" cried the chief lemming when David tumbled

onto his head in a shower of dirt. "Ferrets! Badgers! Run for your lives!"

David was nearly trampled in the sudden mad rush of bodies stampeding up the escape passage. When it was over he stood up and looked around. Off in the distance he could hear the chief lemming crying about ferrets and badgers. But here, which was obviously not outside, there was nothing but another lemming like himself crouching in a corner behind a root.

Nuts, he thought. There'll be heck to pay for this when father finds out. Oh, well, might as well go on out and get a look at outside for all it's going to cost me.

He dropped to all fours and began to pad toward the

exit tunnel. But when he moved, the other lemming cried out in fear.

"No! Please don't hurt me, Mr. Badger."

David stopped. The poor thing was all turned into a ball. It didn't know who he was, and it was shivering with terror.

"I am neither badger nor ferret, whatever they are," he said. "I am a lemming like you, and off to see the outside. My apology if I have disturbed you, I am sure." David liked the sound of that speech. Formal and proper. Confident.

"What?" The other lemming was sniffling. David moved closer. It was a girl!

"I said I'm a lemming, miss. My name is David. What's your name?"

"My name?"

Girls, he thought. They all must be as silly as my sisters.

"Yes, your name!" he thundered (as much as a very young lemming can thunder). "What you are called. Now come out of that ball. You aren't hurt and I am certainly not going to hurt you."

She jumped at the stern tone in his voice. Another nice speech, he thought. First time I've got down below a squeak. He felt rather good about all this.

She uncurled and looked at him. "My name is — Sheba," she said hesitantly. Her eyes widened. "Why, you *are* a lemming."

"That's what I said," snapped David. He was growing impatient.

"And you aren't a badger or a ferret — "

"Also what I said."

"And you come crashing in here and scaring everyone and — what's the matter with you?"

This was a strange turn of events, David thought. The formerly terrified little ball was growing angry. He began to lick his front paws and wash himself.

"What?" he said, thinking not half as well of this answer as his earlier ones.

"You — block-headed, lop-eared, bug-eyed excuse for a lemming! Why would you do something like that to me?"

"To you!" David began to wash himself frantically. He stepped back as she approached. "To you? I didn't even know you were here. I was just trying to dig out to the light."

"Get out of here!" she screamed, her eyes blazing.

"Now listen here," said David, backing up a little faster.

"Out!" she yelled. "O-U-T, out!"

Abandoning every shred of dignity, David turned and ran. He dove for his tunnel and scrambled back to his own burrow. Her angry cries followed him every step of the way.

When he popped out the other side, his father was waiting. It was a long time before he heard the last of it, and to top the whole bad business off, he still hadn't managed to see outside.

For the next few weeks, David was a very well-behaved lemming. His parents thought he had learned his lesson, but they were wrong. He had a new reason for not missing first day outside. That would be Sheba's first day, too.

David was in love.

Two

Finally, the big day came — David's first time outside. He was so excited that he could hardly stand still as his mother licked him clean, explaining over and over again that he must be neat and presentable.

"And, David, you must behave," she said. "Do as the others do, and what you're told. It can be so very dangerous in the field. Don't stray far from the burrow. Listen for me and your father.... "

There was quite a bit more like that. His father had a few things to say, too. David agreed to all of it, but really didn't hear a word. In a few minutes he would actually be outside!

He was first in line behind his father when they (at last!) headed out the doorway. He was quivering with excitement. Then he was *THERE!*

His first impression was that everything was white. But, when his eyes adjusted to the sudden brightness of open daylight, what had begun as disappointment became pure joy. It was everything he had hoped for and more.

For several moments he just stood at the burrow entrance and looked all around and listened to every sound and sniffed at every strange scent. The sky was a breathtaking blue, the grass a marvelous deep green with glistening dewdrops on each spear. The earth was dark, rich brown and smelled of life and goodness. And absolutely everywhere there were lemmings!

Someone bumped him from behind.

"David!" complained one of his brothers. "For goodness' sake plant yourself somewhere else than right in our way. We're hungry even if you aren't!"

David leaped forward, heading for a hill a short distance away. Hungry! How could anyone think of eating at a moment like this? This was to be *experienced!*

His muscles felt as if they had been released from a lifetime in a cramped burrow. He sailed into the air, trying to look everywhere at once at the top of each jump. He had cleared a large tuft of grass on one of these bounds when trouble found him again. He came down on top of the clan chief lemming so hard he quite bowled him over. Being a portly sort, it was a bit of a struggle for the old fellow to get up. There was much yelling about ferrets and badgers and such during the process.

David got out of there fast.

The strange thing, though, he thought as he scampered away, was that he could have sworn he heard Sheba giggle. But that was impossible. The girl thought he was crazy.

Perhaps I am crazy, he thought as he reached the top of the hill and clambered up on a large stone to look around. Or, maybe they are. Look at them down there, ignoring a beautiful day and sticking their heads down in the grass. Feeding their faces when they should be feeding their souls! He rolled over on his back and watched the puffy white clouds pass silently overhead. He stood up on his hind legs and now saw the river.

He couldn't imagine so much dew in one place. He must see this marvelous thing up closer! He began to run back down the hill, this time giving a wide berth to the chief lemming and his family. (There was no sense in stirring up any more fuss, he reasoned.) Even so, as he passed, a thick-jowelled head popped up and gave him a very severe look. He could have sworn once more that he heard a giggle over there. He scooted on by quickly.

He was down on the flat, still some distance from the river, when he heard the alarm cry. Instantly, all around him lemmings bolted for the safety of their holes. David searched about for the trouble, but could see nothing.

"More ferrets and badgers, I suppose," he snorted.

Then he saw the shadow floating across the field. Now that, he thought, is interesting. He jumped toward it.

"David!" cried his mother. "Come into the burrow. You'll be killed! Come quickly!"

But David wouldn't understand. He just kept on chasing the shadow. Soon it became larger. Then he heard a rushing sound above him. He looked up to see a great animal drop out of the very air and pounce on a field mouse not four steps away.

"David!" cried his father. "Run! Run!"

But David thought the animal was beautiful, and sat there in its shadow and watched it eat the mouse. Finished, it made as if to lift in the sky again, spreading its great, wide arms. Then it noticed David. The piercing eyes were fearsome, but they were the clear gold of that morning's sunrise and were very fine.

"Hello," said David. "What is your name?"

The animal tilted his head to one side as he eyed

David curiously. "I am Hawk," it rasped. "And just who —
or should I say what — are you? You look like a lemming,
but you do not act like a lemming."

"And just how should I act?" said David, adding a
respectful "sir."

"Well," said Hawk, "I suppose you should be afraid."

"Afraid?" cried David. "Of a magnificent being such
as you? One might as well fear your home, the sky, for
you are as great as it. Anyone with eyes can see that!"

David thought it his best speech to date. The great
bird merely found it accurate.

"True," it agreed. "You certainly have a good eye, for
a lemming. And courage to match, it seems. And your
name is?"

"David."

"Very well, David. You see clearly. That is something
my brothers admire. Yet courage we admire even more. You
shall have nothing to fear from any of my kind from this
day forth."

With that, Hawk reached forward and raked a claw
across David's forehead. It hurt, but David did not move
to flee as other lemmings would have. Something told
him he would not be killed.

"That mark is pride, David," said Hawk, now lifting
gracefully off the ground on a fresh breeze. "It is a
difficult mark to wear well."

"I will do my best, sir."

"I know you will, David," said Hawk. "Good winds."

"Good winds, sir," said David, having no idea how
one told a good wind from a bad one.

When Hawk had gone, the other lemmings began to pop out of the ground, their eyes wide and shocked looks on their faces. David turned to greet them, sure that they would be envious of his experience and want to know everything that was said. As he was about to relate the tale, he realized no one had approached within twenty steps. They had formed a giant circle about him, and were staring and pointing and whispering among themselves. They parted to let the clan chief lemming through. He looked very upset, yet somehow grimly happy. David began to grow apprehensive.

The chief lemming turned away from David and began to speak:

"You all — except the little ones, of course — know the law. From the day he was birthed, the lemming David has displayed behavior unbecoming one of our clan. He refused the comfort of his burrow and sought to come outside before his time. He would not heed the good cautions of his parents and ran off to the hill without any sense of safety — which is probably what brought Hawk down on us."

Many adults there nodded at that. David didn't like the look of this at all. Even his parents were staring at him as if they didn't know him. Then his heart really fell. Sheba was crying.

"And," the chief lemming went on, "if anyone needed any proof beyond that, he has just provided everything necessary."

He pointed a paw at David.

"He speaks with the enemy and is not harmed! He is

not lemming. He is the one we have feared. The evil one. The one who brings the *madness!*"

David couldn't understand what was happening. What enemy? What madness? The chief lemming stepped close to David, rising to his full height.

"From this day," he said, his voice heavy with importance, "you are not and never have been lemming. You have no mother or father, nor brothers or sisters. No burrow will be open to you, no lemming will speak to you on pain of the same fate."

The chief lemming turned, slowly looking at each one of the assembled. His eyes were dark brown sparks. His voice rang out, full of final authority.

"David the lemming is outcast!" he cried.

As one, all turned their backs on David. All, that is, except Sheba, who looked at him for a moment through tear-stained eyes. Then she, too, joined the others.

Again, almost as one, responding to some communal signal that David could not sense, they drifted off and began to feed. To them, it seemed, David had never even been born.

Three

David's first night alone was very bad. So much had happened that he did not understand. At first he couldn't believe they would all reject him just for speaking to Hawk. He had tried to talk to some of them, but they acted as if he were not there. Next he went to his brothers and sisters. They, too, would not answer. The hardest blow of all was his parents. No matter how he argued, cried, cajoled or complained, neither would acknowledge his presence. He might as well have been talking to a stone for all the response he got.

Finally, he grew angry and stalked off to the top of the hill. If they wouldn't speak to him, he wouldn't speak to them. They'd be sorry, they'd see. But then night came on and all the lemmings went into their safe, warm burrows.

A deep melancholy settled over David. He railed against his impulsive nature; made plans as to how he could change and become a normal lemming. Surely, if he could show them he was like all the rest, they would let him back into the fold.

He got so excited about the idea that he ran down to the burrow and went inside to tell his parents. Halfway down the tunnel he met the lemming who had been his father. He was snarling. He bit David on the nose.

"Go away!" he cried. "Do you want your whole family to become outcast? You were warned to behave. You wouldn't. Now go away!"

David went back up the hill slowly, his spirits

dashed. The night was deeper now. There was a chilly breeze. He found a sun-warmed niche out of the wind (now he knew at least one kind of bad wind) and cried himself to sleep. His dreams were punctuated with soft whimpers, and shivering. Several times he came groggily awake. Once he thought it was because something large had brushed a nearby bush. Then the wind shook the limbs, making a crisp noise. David looked around a bit, his heart pounding in his chest. Nothing moved that the wind did not move. He snuggled a little deeper in his niche and eventually drifted back to sleep.

When the warm sun woke him in the morning, he was cheered a bit. The field was rippling with sweet grass and young lemmings. It looked to be another beautiful day. He washed himself and hopped off the stone to nibble at some nearby grass.

Several times that day he saw Sheba, grazing with a group of lemmings. Each time his mood fell a little more.

He wished he could talk to her, but he didn't try. If what her father (and his own!) had said was true, he wouldn't risk causing Sheba this kind of problem. Being outcast would be even harder on her than him, he supposed. Besides her family, she had friends. In the short time he had been alive, David hadn't made any of those.

Well, that was just as well. Nobody for him to miss that much as long as he didn't think about his parents and Sheba. And, come right down to it, they all thought he was crazy, anyway. Even Sheba, it seemed.

So, as this and the days to follow went by, David grew slowly resigned to his fate. Gradually, he began to behave less and less like a lemming. Largely because it was painful to see Sheba and not be able to speak to her, he took to feeding at night and sleeping in the daytime. It was good that he did, for he had been lucky his first nights out. After dark the field and the hill were dangerous places to be.

There *were* such things as badgers and ferrets. And others like the mink and the fox. Hungry things stalked the night trails. The sky, at least, was safe. The hunting birds — Hawk's brothers — left him alone because of the mark on his forehead. Some, though, came very close before they swerved away, looking back over their shoulders in disbelief.

But when the walking hunters approached, his mark was of no use. There was more than one time when David wished he could become just another lemming and spend these dark hours curled up next to the warmth and safety of family and friends. He could have dug a burrow of his own beneath the stone, of course. But David had a quality that one often finds with courage, though usually it is not to be admired as much. David was just plain stubborn. Even after many nights in the open, when he had grown at last truly aware of his jeopardy there, he felt no inclination to change his ways.

Not that it was all bad for him. Sometimes his naturally curious nature pushed the fear and loneliness back — for the night was beautiful to him. The moon was entrancing. He spent endless hours staring at its face. Its changing shape was a curiosity; and the way it flew so slowly across the sky. It must have great dark wings, this bird, to catch the high winds above where even Hawk could go!

Sometimes, he would talk to it. Sometimes, he sang little songs to it as he grazed in the silvery light. It did not answer. Probably too far away to hear a little lemming. He kept on as the mood struck him. It helped — a little.

And some nights, when the air was very clear and quiet, the sky would explode with twinkling lights. Of all lemmings, he was sure he was the first to see these. He wondered how they lifted up from the river where he had seen them during the day. It was a puzzle.

It was in contemplation of these one evening in midsummer that he lost himself and so did not hear the approaching footfalls. He was not disturbed until he felt the hot breath on his neck. Startled, he looked around.

His heart stopped. Towering over him like some gigantic evil tree was the most fearsome creature he had ever heard of, let alone seen. It was Wolf.

The swollen tongue hung loosely from Wolf's huge jaws. His eyes were green slits. He panted lightly as he studied David. He bent forward, his teeth glinting in the moon's light.

"What is this?" he said in a very deep voice.

"My n-name is David, s-sir," stuttered the lemming.

"I know what a lemming is," said Wolf, "which is what you certainly look like. Is a 'David' something else?"

"No, s-sir. I am a lemming."

The beast regarded him. There was blood and a tuft of brown fur on his jowls. He had just had a fat rabbit.

"I have never seen a lemming out with the night people. Have you lost your way?"

The first terrible fright had passed. Though he was still scared, it seemed the animal was not going to eat him immediately. But, what should he do? He needed time to think. He sat on his haunches and began to lick his paws and wash his face. That's when he felt the scar on his forehead and was instantly ashamed. How would Hawk think of him, standing here tongue-tied, weak-kneed and stuttering like some mere ... lemming? His wits began to return. Well, he thought, I can't outrun or out-fight him. I'll have to outtalk him. He will probably eat me in the end anyway, but he will know he's been in a scrap!

"Lost my way?" said David, stretching up to his full

height — which was just a little above Wolf's paw —
and continuing to wash himself. "Why, not at all. It is
my custom to enjoy the evening after dinner. The fields
are pleasant at night, don't you agree?"

"Ahhh," sighed Wolf. His muzzle curved into a grin
that was half astonishment. "He walks the fields after
dinner."

"A pleasant excursion that settles the meal," said
David.

Wolf tipped his head back and laughed.

"Sir!" snapped David. "If there is humor here I see it
not."

Wolf laughed again, then caught himself. "Your
pardon — uh, David, is it? Yes. Well, no insult was intended, I assure you. It is just that I have lived many
years and walked many miles. I thought there was
nothing more to discover. You give me hope."

"Well, then," said David, his heart beginning to beat
again. "No offense intended, none taken is my policy."

He felt a strange power, a giddiness. He felt reckless.
How far could this go? He stared at the great animal, at
the twin moons that shone in its eyes. A strange idea
crept into his brain.

"And have you had your dinner this evening, sir?" he
asked.

Wolf nodded slowly. "Why, yes, David, I have."

"Then," said David, taking the plunge, "perhaps you
would care to join me in my stroll. You would be most
welcome."

Wolf was quiet for a moment. Then his shaggy head

began to shake slowly from side to side. Yet he said: "David, I believe I would consider it an honor to walk with you."

"Then, let's be off, sir. A glorious evening is wasting away!"

Wolf laughed. "And where, young David, are we going?"

"To the top of the hill, of course. There is a moon to serenade, my good Wolf!"

"You sing, too?"

"The highest of arts, I should think," said David, setting off up the path.

"I should have known," said Wolf softly. "Somehow, I should have known."

"What's that?" called David, pausing to look back. In truth, he had heard every word.

"What? Oh ... I said I should have known, ah, that we would be going up the hill."

He really was quite polite, thought David. He liked Wolf.

"If there is somewhere else you would prefer, good Wolf, then name it. But, do make up your mind. The moon is well up and these short legs of mine make long work of hills."

Wolf smiled gently. It was an astonishing accomplishment for that ferocious face. He glanced upwards.

"You are right, David. We are late, and I have been the cause of it." He looked back at David. "Perhaps you will allow me to make up for it by giving you a lift. It will save time, and besides, it is well known that the strain of climbing is not good for the digestion."

"Why, Wolf!" exclaimed David. "That is most gracious of you, indeed!"

With that, Wolf dropped to his stomach. David hopped up and gained a purchase in the deep fur at the great animal's shoulders. And off they went.

The sight of the lemming riding the wolf was reported by so many of the night people that thereafter no fox or ferret or badger dared attack the strange lemming with the face mark. But that was not what brought the night people on such long journeys to the field in the weeks to follow. It was the spectacle of Wolf and David performing their strange harmonies there on the hill, joining together in fellowship of song with each moon.

That, no one believed until they saw it for themselves.

Some didn't even believe it then.

Four

The strange thing about it all, thought David as he was resting on his rock in the warm summer sunshine, was that with all his accomplishments he was still outcast. What lemming could claim experiences so grand as his? What lemming could walk the night paths alone? There were none, and all knew it.

Why should he of all lemmings be considered unworthy? It puzzled and frustrated him. And as much as he tried to deny it to himself, it hurt. He was, after all, a lemming. No matter how independent he seemed, and no matter how many friends he had among the other peoples, he needed his own kind. But they refused him. Why?

One evening after song he had broached the subject with his friend, Wolf. Wolf had looked at him and nodded sympathetically.

"David," he had said, "do you know what a 'far walker' is?"

"A term for one of your people is it not, Wolf?"

"Yes, David, we had one. But it is not a common thing. A far walker appears only once in many generations, and only when a great need occurs. My people have not seen one since the most ancient of days when the ice covered these lands and those far to the south. It was a time of great hunger and death.

"Our legends tell us that the people were lost among the great mountains of ice, confused by the snow that fell even in summer. And they were starving. It was then a far walker appeared, whispering in each ear that one should grasp the tail of the next. In this manner he formed the people into a great line. Then, taking the lead, he brought them through to safety. It was a long and terrible journey, and many died along the way. But some survived, and all knew our race owed its continued existence to the far walker."

"He must have been a great wolf," said David. "A leader of leaders."

Wolf shook his head. "That is the strangest thing of all. When the people came out of the snow, far to the south, they discovered the far walker was one who had been driven from the pack because he could not hunt. He was one of the least of us, David."

It was David's turn to shake his head. "Led to safety by a lame wolf," he said. "That is amazing."

"I did not say he was lame, David."

"But, you said he was driven from the pack. If not for lameness, then what?"

"He was blind, David."

David sat in a stunned silence. Finally he said: "But, how? When even the sighted couldn't find a way."

"That, I do not know. But it is said that ever after the far walker was the greatest hunter of all. That he could find game in the darkest of nights and run it down through the thickest of forests without difficulty." Wolf paused. "There are some who believe he saw through his dreams, though how that could be I cannot say."

A wolf who could not see, yet did. Who could not hunt, and then could. David asked Wolf if he knew what had happened to cause such a thing.

"All that is known is that after he had been driven away he wandered, near starvation, for a very long time. Eventually, he found himself on a mountainside — "

"How could he know?" interrupted David.

"By the cry of one who lives only there," said Wolf. "And knowing that, he decided to seek out the highest of the high places and throw himself to his death.

"After many days' travel he reached the high places and made ready to end his life. He sang the first song that is the last song, the birth song that is the death song. It was then that something took place and though still blind he could see more clearly than any wolf that lived."

Wolf fell silent.

"Why did he return to help your people?" asked David. "They had driven him out."

He had almost said "outcast."

Wolf shook his head thoughtfully. "That seems strange to you only because much the same has happened to you very recently. The far walker knew that the company of one's own is as important as blood and air. And he knew that even should they not accept him back, he must do what he could for them. The first law is the survival of your race, David. It is important even over your own life."

"And did they accept him?"

Wolf nodded. "With honor and respect. And he held no rancor for them. It is said that throughout his long life afterwards he treated all with kindness and reverence. That there grew to be around him an aura of wisdom and grace."

Wolf fell silent, his tale finished. David thought about the story, wondering if he could show such forgiveness to those who had made him outcast; if he would bother to help those who had hurt him. A picture of all the lemmings grazing peacefully in the sweet grass came to him. There was Sheba. And mother. And father. And the old clan chief.

"Why did you tell me this?" he said.

Wolf looked at him for a long time. David was almost convinced he would receive no answer at all when Wolf finally said: "I think that among your people, David, you may be a far walker."

David looked out across the field of moonlit grass. Another picture entered his mind. That of a half-starved blind wolf singing his death song to the highest winds.

His voice was as heavy as the weight on his heart when he spoke.

"And if I do not want this burden?" he said, simply.

Wolf did not look at David, nor did he answer.

He opened his great muzzle and sent a cry of lament towards the setting moon.

Five

The next morning, David sat at the riverbank, waiting for the river stars to appear. But, it was not these that captured his deepest thoughts this day. It was Wolf's words of the night before. How could a lemming — even one so odd as himself — ever be a far walker?

If nothing else, his legs were too short, and that was a fact! It was ridiculous when one thought about it in the broad light of day. But, just supposing he were one. What was the disaster that was about to happen? Wolf had said, after all, that far walkers only appear at times of great need. He looked around at the lemmings grazing in the field. Except for a bit of a shortage of grass that was forcing them to feed farther from their burrows than usual, there was no desperate fate awaiting them that he could see. No mountains of ice. No great plague. No terrible flood.

A nearby noise distracted him. He glanced in that direction and saw a group of young lemmings grazing. Sheba was among them. He wondered how it was that she stood out so clearly from the others.

She was smaller than some, larger than others. Her form was as a lemming's should be, her color the same, too. But there was something about the way the sunlight caught her fur, the way the morning breeze ruffled her coat like the wind on a field of sweet grass.

For a moment, he had an urge to speak to her. To try to explain. Then he put the thought from his mind. As much as he would like to, he wouldn't risk it at the price of having her named outcast, too. She probably wouldn't talk to him anyway. He had insulted her own father — twice.

Somewhere down deep, the old hurt began. Thoughts of Sheba always seemed to heighten his isolation. He got off his haunches and padded toward his hill. The river stars were forgotten. The lemmings made way for him as he ascended the slope, not even bothering to stop their munching. He suspected they were afraid of him, which was probably why they left his hilltop grass alone even though it was the last good grazing around.

Maybe that was his job as far walker for the lemmings, he mused. To keep them from eating themselves to death!

At the top of the hill, he went to his sleeping stone. The sun had been up long enough to warm it, so he clambered up and lay down. For a long time he gazed at the mountains, far to the east. When he finally dozed off, his dreams were full of Sheba and Hawk and Wolf singing strange songs in the high places.

It was well after dark when he awoke. The night was clear and cool. Wolf was sitting on his haunches next to the stone. "Good evening, David," he said as the lemming sat up and began to wash himself. "You are well?"

David said hello, but nothing more. A silence as deep as the night fell between them. The moon rose, but David did not feel like singing. Wolf did not press the matter. He sat silently, waiting.

For a very long time David looked at the hill and the field. He thought about the lemmings curled up snugly in their burrows — and about Sheba. A night wind came up, riffling through the grass and turning the hillside into a gentle river of wind waves. He let his gaze follow one of the waves eastward. When it disappeared into the darkness, his eyes swept upwards to the mountains.

Their snowy peaks stood stark against the black fabric of the sky. They looked cold, and so very far away.

"What do you think I might find up there, Wolf?" he said, finally.

"I walk far, David, but I am not a far walker."

"The answer, perhaps?"

"An answer, perhaps. What is it you seek to know?"

David thought about that. "What makes me so different. How I can be — accepted. Why I was born."

"There can be a danger to such questions, David."

David looked at Wolf. "You mean I might not like the answers?"

Wolf nodded, but said nothing.

"There is no hope for me here. Not with things the way they are now," said David. He was thinking of Sheba. He looked again at the far mountains. "Perhaps there."

"Perhaps," said Wolf. He stood up and stretched the kinks out of his powerful legs. "You might even find some of what you seek along the way. Some of my journeys have taught me more than what I found at the end. When will you leave?"

"Now is as good a time as any," said David.

"I will walk with you a ways," said Wolf.

But they had not taken a single step when with a

rustle of dry grass Sheba suddenly appeared. Even in the moonlight her fear of Wolf was evident. She was shaking as though chilled to the bone.

"What!" cried David.

She did not look at him; her eyes were fastened on Wolf.

"Who is this?" said Wolf.

"I-I, my name is...." She couldn't speak.

"It's Sheba! Wolf, it's Sheba!"

Wolf bent forward and down to peer at her. "Is she sick, David?"

David suddenly laughed, then just as suddenly flushed with anger at himself. He knew exactly how she felt. He quickly moved next to her and touched her shoulder with a paw.

"Wolf is a friend," he said, as soothingly as possible. Then, to Wolf, "She's afraid."

Wolf nodded. "I understand. I won't go far."

He turned and was gone. It was an astonishingly quiet departure considering his bulk. David, unable to think of anything comforting to say, simply continued to stroke her fur. Gradually, her shivering began to subside, and she was able to turn her wide eyes to him.

Even in her fear, she was beautiful. The moon seemed to be singing along the spines of her soft fur. It was marvelous being this close to her. David wished time could be stopped right here and now.

Yet, after a while, she was calm enough to speak.

"David!" she whispered, "He is terrible!"

David shook his head. "No. He just seems that way to you. He is one of the few friends I have in this world."

She blinked. "I've seen you with him when I could slip away from my parents. But he's so much larger up close. Those teeth, those eyes. I never imagined!"

David stopped stroking her. "Sheba! Your parents! If they find out you've come out here at night — if they discover you've talked to me — you'll be outcast, too. You must go back, right now!"

He began to push her away, but she resisted.

"No, David. I-I'm here. I had to come. To find out."

David stopped. "Find out? Find out what?"

She seemed to gather her courage again. "About you, about us. But I heard you talking just now. You're — going away, aren't you?"

David sighed. "I don't know. Maybe they are right about me."

"It's true then? You are going?"

David waved his paw, taking in the clearing. "What have I here?" His paw dropped helplessly to his side.

She moved very close to him.

"You have me," she said, simply.

He didn't believe his ears. A pain stabbed through him.

"No!" he said.

She stepped back, a puzzled look on her face. "Oh, no! I was wrong. You don't feel about me the way I feel about you. Oh, this is terrible!"

"Wait!" cried David. "I do! I always have, from the first! I thought you hated me. You turned away."

Her head dropped. "Yes. I did. I'm sorry. It was cowardly of me, David. I am truly sorry."

She turned as if to leave.

"Don't go," he said.

She looked at him. Hope filled her eyes.

"I wasn't wrong, then," she said, tentatively holding out a paw. As if in a magical dream, David took it in his. They were quiet for a long time. Then David spoke:

"Yes, I'm going. I can't explain why, but I am."

"Are you saying that I wouldn't understand, David?"

"No. I'm saying that I don't understand, either."

After a moment, she said, "Then I'll go with you."

David looked deeply at her. "No. Please don't misunderstand me, but you can't. I don't know where I'm going or why."

She scowled. "It's because I'm a girl, isn't it?"

David took her other paw in his. "No, that isn't it. Not long ago, you would have been right. I thought like that, about girls, I mean. I was wrong."

"Then, what is it, David?"

Looking at her, David wondered how he could explain something he himself didn't understand. How do you put in words something that is just there in your heart?

"Do you love me?" he asked without really knowing why.

She frowned, but said, "Yes."

"Why?" he asked.

Her frown deepened. "Why? Why do I love you? What kind of a question is that?"

He did not reply. He didn't know what to say.

"Oh," she said, suddenly. "It's the same thing, isn't it?"

David realized she was right. It made him proud that they had come to understand something together.

"Yes," he said, "I think it is the same. One of those things you can't explain. It just is."

She nodded slowly, sadly. She glanced off in the direction Wolf had gone.

"When?" she asked.

"Tonight," he answered.

There was a silence between them, then David said, "I don't know when I'll return, or even if I will."

She looked away, and said, "It isn't fair."

"No," agreed David, lamely.

She turned back to him and, leaning forward, brushed her muzzle against his.

"Goodbye," she whispered, and was gone.

David was staring into the night after her and didn't notice Wolf's return. After a time Wolf said, "So, there are two lemmings with courage. Did you ask her to wait for you?"

"No," said David.

"That is best," said Wolf. "One that strong would have her own mind, anyway. Her heart will guide her."

I hope so, thought David. I truly hope so.

The moon cast its soft glow in front of them as the wolf and the lemming moved off the crown of the hill and headed towards the far mountains. In a little while they disappeared into the shadows, and were gone.

The following morning, if the lemmings noticed David was not asleep on his stone, they did not mention it in conversation. For the next several days one lemming, a soft-furred female, went part way up the hill and paused and sniffed the air as if searching for something. But then she stopped coming; and even when the grazing became terrible elsewhere, nobody went to the top of the hill after that.

Six

The next evening, when David awoke, Wolf was gone. He was probably hunting. They had traveled far that first night, crossing a great distance of field and scrub before stopping some ways into the forest. David had been so tired, and it had been so dark, that he had not cared to even consider his surroundings. Now he looked around with wonder, and with some fear.

Even Wolf's fine talent at description had not prepared him for this. Up till now a tree to David was a riverbank willow. But these! Their trunks were as large as the whole top of the hill. From the ground to where the first limbs began was the length of a good after-dinner stroll. His eyes were drawn upwards. He leaned farther and farther back, searching for the tops, until he tipped over backwards with a thud.

"Well," said Wolf, emerging from a nearby shadow. "You are not going to make much of a far walker if you cannot even stand up!"

David flushed beneath his soft brown fur. He got quickly to his feet and began to wash himself. After he had regained some measure of composure, he cautiously leaned back again.

"My," he said, "but they are big. And very strange."

"I am afraid," said Wolf, "that you will get very used to them before you pass beyond the forest."

"Then it is far to the other side?"

"Two days' fast trot for me. Much longer for those short legs of yours."

————————————————

Even in the near night, David could see for some distance along their way. On and on the giants marched without end. It would be very difficult maintaining the proper direction night or day in this place. Without Wolf's help, he was sure he would lose his way.

"Perhaps," said Wolf, "we could save some time."

David looked at him. "You mean I could ride."

Wolf nodded.

David thought about that. Finally, he said: "No, I think not. If a far walker I am, then a far walker I must be."

Wolf nodded again. "I thought you would say something like that."

"You think I am stubborn?"

"Yes," said Wolf, laughing. "It is one of the things I like most about you, David."

David laughed, too. This place, for all the danger it might hold, was of little consequence to one with a friend like Wolf at his side. He had nothing to fear. Shortly after he had eaten some grass, they set off through the now totally dark forest. Though he knew there was a full moon somewhere far above, David saw no evidence of it. The great trees were so plentiful, and their branches so intertwined, that not even an occasional stray beam survived to the ground. Yet wolves are night people, and lemmings live in dark burrows. Both do quite nicely in very dim places.

Just as a faint light began to relieve the gloom, they stopped to rest. Wolf led the way to a tumbling stream, and near it they bedded down for the day. When David awoke to his second night in the forest he was surprised to see Wolf silhouetted in a patch of moonlight. For a moment, he thought he was back at the field, and that he had been dreaming about the journey. Then he realized it was the break in the trees caused by the stream. Well, that was good, at least. As long as they were near it, they would have some light.

Now he noticed there was something strange about the way Wolf was standing. He was tense. His muscles were quivering along his back, rippling his fur like the wind on grass. His ears were pointing sharply forward. A low growl rumbled briefly somewhere deep in his chest.

David called to him, but he did not answer.

"Wolf!" said David, more forcefully. "What is it? Is there trouble?"

"David," said Wolf, glancing quickly at him. "I must go. An old enemy has returned to my pack."

David could not believe his ears. How could he continue without Wolf? "An enemy? Who could be an enemy of yours?"

"This is one of my own kind, David. He was a bad, quarrelsome wolf. I shouldn't have to tell you that those of your own kind can very often be the worst of enemies."

"But, how shall I go on? I will be lost. Who will protect me?"

Wolf looked hard at David, yet his voice was soft when he spoke. "Who protected you from Hawk? And from me on that first night?"

David was ashamed. Wolf was his friend. He wouldn't

leave if the matter were of little importance. And this was, after all, David's journey. Wolf had been more than kind to accompany him this far.

"You are right," he said. "It was cowardly of me to speak so."

"Don't confuse fear with cowardice, David. We are all afraid at times. Courage is what you do in spite of fear. You have more courage than most."

Wolf's ears pricked up once more. For a moment he looked intently to the north.

"I have little time," he said. "But there is advice I must give you, so listen closely. I have brought us to this stream because I feared something like this might happen. You must follow the stream to its source, a great lake. This you will have to cross. Do not try to circle it. It is far too long for that. Even should you manage to overcome all the dangers that lie along its shores, it would surely be winter before you returned to the falls, for they lie directly across from the stream's headwaters. And at the top of these is the path to the highest of the high places.

"I will try to return and help you before you get that far, but I can promise nothing. The pack is far to the north, and my enemy is surely stronger now. He was little more than a pup when I drove him off, but there has been much time for him to grow."

"I will be fine, I am sure," said David, with more bravado than he felt.

"That I believe, David. But, be quiet now, because I have more to tell. There are many who would wish you ill in this forest. The greater part of these are night people, so I think you should travel by day from now on. Still, you must be wary of those of Hawk's brotherhood who may not have heard of your mark, and of the several walking hunters. Of these, watch most carefully for Lynx. His claws are death.

"You may recognize him by his great ears, which have tufts of fur at their tips. But I fear if you are close enough to see these, you will be through. So, watch the shadows carefully. His coat is spots and stripes, and if you are both observant and lucky, you may avoid him."

"And if I am seen first?"

"Then, except for one chance, you are lost. The great cats despise water. Lynx most of all. Stay near the stream and make use of that if you can."

Wolf's ears lifted again. He trembled. "There is so much more you need to know. There are hunters who fly and those who walk — and some who neither fly nor walk. But I have time to warn you of only one more. That is Eagle. His domain is the land beyond the lake. The way to the high places. He is of Hawk's tribe, but that is like saying the sun is of the tribe of stars."

"How will I know him?"

"You will know him. He flies higher and sees farther than any of the brotherhood."

"Has he a weakness?"

"Not to my knowledge. He is proud and arrogant, and has reason to be so. But perhaps a far walker can find a way."

Wolf's ears pricked up a third time.

"I must go," he said.

"Go, then, and with my thanks," said David.

"Fare well, far walker!" cried Wolf. "May the spoor be fresh!"

"And your kill swift!" David answered in the ritual parting of the wolf people.

Wolf was gone in an instant, his gray form sliding like a shadow's shadow out of the moonlight and off into the trees. David was suddenly very alone. Around him, the soft night noises took on an alarming quality. Far above, the wind sighing through the branches sounded like the cry of a dying animal. The night seemed to come alive and press in upon him. Though the air was warm, he began to shiver. He wished he were back in the field on his warm hill stone, watching Sheba grazing peacefully below. But he wasn't, and would never be if he didn't keep going. So he set off along the stream bank, his legs like stone and his wide eyes darting toward every rustling leaf.

As he traveled, intending to try to make a few miles before resting for the night, something Wolf had said came back again and again to haunt him:

"...and some who neither fly nor walk."

What such a thing could be worried David all that night. When he had curled up in an old log and turned his back to the fearful forest, it disturbed his sleep. A strange, evil thing was behind him in his dreams.

A thing that neither walked nor flew.

Seven

David was very tired when he awoke in the morning. A bad rest and the switching around of his waking and sleeping hours had done it to him. But his basically cheerful nature came to the fore when he found a tasty bunch of deep woods grass and had his breakfast. Though still quite gloomy, and certainly nothing like the field in daylight, the forest was nevertheless a far less threatening place now. He set off up the stream feeling something akin to hope.

For a while, the going was easy. A bit of a spring infused his stride. At this rate, he would be making much better time than Wolf would have imagined possible. He began to feel he might make the lake that very day, or at the latest the next. Then he came to a second stream, and his hopes were dashed.

Entering from the north, its flow cut the bank of the main channel in half. David didn't even consider trying to swim it. It was much too fast for him. With less bounce in his step, he turned north. He would have to follow the feeder until he found a crossing. With luck there would be a fallen log not too far away. Otherwise, he might have to walk to its very headwaters.

The way was up, through a tangle of thick brush and vines. The farther he went, the worse it got. Several times he had to skirt thickets so dense he didn't think a bug could get through. Then he came to yet another feeder stream.

If this keeps up, he thought wearily, I'll soon run into myself from behind!

Doggedly, he set off along the new rill. It was quite short, however, ending in a beautiful hillside spring. He stopped there to rest among the soft ferns, drank his fill and listened for a bit to the chattering of a small bird in a berry bush. He had grown quite hot during the climb, and it was pleasant to be by the spring.

Twenty minutes later he was back at the large feeder, continuing up what soon became a steep-walled canyon. This was a jumble of huge boulders through which the stream flowed, and it made for quite a job for David. It was midday when he reached the upper end of the draw, clambered up on a large stone and saw a delta. He immediately felt it was his best chance.

The stream, through some quirk of nature, broke into five smaller flows as it passed through a small valley. Above the valley, it reassembled itself and entered another canyon. If he were to cross, this would have to be the place. From where he stood, the little branches looked fordable to David, except for one. But it had a log jam, and so might offer crossing potential there.

He hopped off the boulder and ran down to the first branch. It was just a trickle. He crossed it easily. The second one was a bit deeper, but he found a boulder that served his purpose. Using it as a single stepping stone, he made it to the far bank.

Now he scampered quickly to the middle branch and saw that his fears had been justified. It was way over his head, and as swift as wind. He headed upstream, toward the log jam. In a soft spot, he lost his footing and fell in a hole. Thinking himself a clumsy fool, he got up and started to move on. Then, he stopped. There had been something strange about that hole. He walked back to study it.

It wasn't a hole. It was a footprint. What Wolf called a "spoor." A chill went down his back. He looked quickly around. Forcing himself into a semblance of calm, he checked to see if he could determine which direction the animal had been heading. With a start, he realized the tracks went directly toward the way he had come. And, by the sharp, unweathered edge to their outlines, perhaps not long ago.

Why hadn't he seen anything?

Of course! The detour up the little feeder stream. An animal this large would simply step over that little riffle. He shivered. How close he had come! He felt a definite need to cross that center branch and get out of there.

The gravel bar was far too exposed for his liking. Though it was probably just nerves, he suddenly had the feeling that he was being watched. He headed quickly for the jam. He reached it in a matter of minutes and began to work his way through the jumble to the stream side. He glanced back at the gravel bar several times, but saw nothing. Still, his hackles were on edge. To save time, he tried to avoid a circuitous path along one log and back down the other. But his leap was short, and he fell down into the jam.

He felt pain. Suddenly it hurt to put weight on his

right front paw. With his good paw, he pushed aside a stick and squeezed out onto a jutting log. At the end of it, he saw it wasn't long enough. He would never be able to leap the distance to the far bank. He had to find another way. He turned around and saw Lynx.

There was no mistaking him. The coat was as Wolf had described. The ears were far too large for the head, and they were tufted.

David dove for the deepest part of the jam. Perhaps the tangle would protect him.

He soon found that it would not. Within seconds, Lynx was tearing at the jam, his great claws and legs snapping drift that was twice as thick as David was tall.

David backed away until he could back no farther. There was no escape. He couldn't leave the jam or Lynx would have him. If he stayed, it was just a matter of time.

Now, Lynx began to break through. David squeezed against the dead wood at his back. There was a cracking sound. He popped outside. He looked around. He was trapped. On three sides there was the stream. In front, Lynx. He was on a log that jutted out into the flow. There was nowhere else to go. He backed out to the end.

An ear-splitting snarl issued from the jam. It scared him so badly he almost fell into the stream. Lynx had seen him. With a thud that shook the whole jam, the cat slammed against the near wall. He screamed again, in pain. In his anger, it did not occur to Lynx to simply go back out the way he had come, hop over the pile and take David. Instead, he exploded against the tangle. Sticks, limbs and slabs of wood flew in every direction, some of them landing in the stream. For the hundredth time, David looked for an escape. There was none.

The stream was too swift. He couldn't run as fast as those slabs of wood were floating.

Slabs of wood! Wood floats!

Lynx was almost through. There was no other choice. David jumped. He didn't land cleanly, but he got his

claws into a passing chunk of bark. Sore paw or not, he was not about to lose hold.

After some chancy scrabbling, he pulled himself up. By the time he felt secure enough to glance back at the jam, he was rounding a far downstream corner. It was then that Lynx broke through and discovered David was gone. The great cat's cry of rage and frustration should have scared the wits out of David, but it didn't. He was suddenly feeling rather good about himself.

"Wood floats," he said out loud. He began to giggle, then broke into a laughing fit.

"Wood floats," he sang, "and not old goats and who will tote poor Lynx's oats?"

His silly song, interspersed with laughter, echoed off the canyon walls as he floated merrily along. He wasn't the least bit concerned about tomorrow.

Today had turned out just fine.

Eight

The trip downstream was pure delight. The water bounced and bubbled and chattered happily. Little clouds of four-winged insects the color of old roses lifted from the overhanging shrubbery. Dancing in intricate patterns they flickered through the slanting rays of late afternoon like clusters of tiny stars. Now and then one would flit too close to the water and be sucked in by a hungry trout. David began to hum quietly. There was music here. He sang:

> Far hillsides calling, weaving golden
> Mysteries to me
> Of journeys undertaken with
> No end in sight to see.
>
> Far valleys filled with mist and sun
> And memories to be
> Are calling, calling, calling, calling
> On the wind to me.
>
> I must be off. Stay! Hold me not!
> I've much to see and do
> Before returning with the sun
> To burrow, home and you . . .
> Before returning with the sun
> To burrow, home and you.

Not bad, thought David. Not that bad, at all. He might just make a decent far walker yet. Of course, he would have to try the song out on Wolf the first chance he got. Wolf knew about far hillsides and wind messages and such. He would judge the work fairly.

David turned his attention to his present situation. The slab had passed the little secondary feeder some time back, so he would soon be approaching the main stream. At the moment, he had no idea as to how he might gain the proper shore, or even if he could make land at all. He might be swept right out into the main flow. That could be quite uncomfortable.

He decided to jump for the correct bank as soon as he got an opportunity. For far longer than he would have wished, that chance did not come. In fact, up until the last moment, he thought it wouldn't come at all. But just before the feeder entered the main stream, it widened into a swift, deep pool. David's slab was picked up by an odd turn of current, an eddy, and in the end he was swept within inches of the shore. He hardly got his feet wet as he hopped off.

The shriek startled him so he stumbled and fell in the mud. He scrambled up and froze. There, on the far bank, was Lynx. The cat screamed again and again. For a moment, David thought he was a dead lemming. Then he remembered Wolf's words.

Lynx hated water.

He should be safe, then. But that screaming was terrible. Lynx seemed angry enough to forget his hatred of the water.

David got out of there, fast.

The piercing cries subsided as he moved upstream. He felt better and better as he went along. Luck was with him. He walked far into the night, and not once during that time did he hear or see anything that seemed in the least dangerous. Not until late the next morning did his energy flag. Just before noon he came to a place where the stream curved around a sunny knoll covered with sweet grass.

He had not eaten since the day before, so he stopped there to feed. Afterwards he found a soft mound of dirt just above the stream and lay down to rest. It was a most pleasant place, this sunny little island of light in the middle of the dark forest. Soon, he grew drowsy, and soon after that he dozed off.

* * *

"What isss thisss?" asked the voice in his dream. "Isss it a sssquirrel? Doesss it bite?"

David's eyes popped open. He froze.

With ever the faintest rustle, it slid out of the shadows, curving towards him through the streamside grass. Before David could even consider making a run for it, it had blocked off any chance of escape into the forest. All that was left was the stream, and David was no match for that swift current. He was trapped.

"It isss a sssstrange sssquirrel, thisss one thinksss. Isss it dead?"

Wolf's words, the ones that had haunted David, came to him again: "...and some who neither fly nor walk."

This thing neither flew nor walked.

And it was enormous! A shiny, slimy, black worm. An evil head with slitted eyes, connected to a horrible undulating tube of a stomach. Slowly, it circled David, enclosing him in a loop. Now, the loops began to pile up one on another. Four, then five, then six coils curled about him until he lay in a terrible whirlpool of rippling black skin. Then the movement ceased.

"Yesss. It isss breathing. It isss playing posssum. Thisss one hasss nothing to fear from it. Thisss one can eat it, yesss."

The shadow of the head began to grow on the ground in front of David. He had to do something soon or he would be bleached bones left in a trail of grass. His body shook. He tried to force himself to stay still, but he could not. Suddenly he realized *he* hadn't moved. The ground had! The soft mound of earth was a mole hill! The owner must be digging nearby.

The shadow was larger. A drop of saliva spattered to the ground very near his head. It would only take a short time to break through to the tunnel. But if he attempted an obvious escape, he was sure he would be dead in *half* a short time. He had to distract the thing.

He sat up quickly and let out a loud "WHOOOEEE!!!"

The shadow froze.

David tried to do it again, but this time it was half screech and half squeak because his first clear look at the horrible death's head suspended over him almost cost him control of his voice. Nevertheless, the head jerked back farther, its forked tongue flicking in and out nervously. Fighting against his fear, David made as if he had just noticed the animal.

"Oh, sorry," he said. "I didn't mean to startle you, I am sure. But I must keep the voice in shape. Far walkers are singers, too, you know."

"Far walkersss? Sssingersss?"

The slit-eyed head gained a wrinkled brow. David began to wash himself, hoping that the motion would cover up what he was doing with his back feet: carefully scratching away at the soft mound beneath.

"Yes, of course," he said. "Far walkers. You know, walking. Legs."

Well, now, he thought, that's monumentally stupid. This thing doesn't have legs. He tried another tack.

"Traveling. Going from one place to another. I am on a journey, Mr., uh, you didn't mention your name."

"SSSNAKE!" it spat, arching its vile face so close to David's that the flicking tongue swatted his nose.

David fought an almost uncontrollable urge to panic and run. But he didn't move from his spot. The earth had just settled a little beneath him. How far, he wondered? Would he have time? He rushed on, saying anything that came into his head.

"Singing is the highest art according to Wolf, you know."

The head jerked back and darted from side to side. The tongue tested the air busily.

"Wolf! Isss that one here? Thisss one doesss not like Wolf. Wolf bitesss, yesss!"

With Snake distracted, David had a chance. He dropped to all fours and began to tear at the soft earth. He was close, so close. The earth settled again. He lost his balance. When he looked up, Snake's head was very still, and the yellow eyes were fixed on him.

"That one isss not here," it said. "And thisss one thinksss there isss no sssuch thingsss as far walkersss sssingersss."

It was going to attack! David needed more time!

"Oh, certainly there is!" he squeaked. "Singing. I shall sing something for you."

But what? Every song he had ever known had gone right out of his head. Everything but an old nursery rhyme that was nothing but silly verses repeating themselves in a tuneless singsong. But it was all he had, so he began it:

Go to sleep, go to sleep
Little lemming, you're keeping
All the sheep, all the sheep
From the sweetest grass around.

Night is here, there's no fear,
All the others are near.
Night is here, there's no fear,
All the others are near.

Snake's head began to sway slowly. The yellow eyes glazed over. The tongue hung suddenly slack from the fanged jaws. It was such a startling transformation that for a moment, David forgot to continue digging. Worse yet, he forgot to continue singing. The light of awareness began to return to Snake's vicious face.

David had no idea what had happened. But he did know that if he didn't stop gawking and take advantage of the situation he would be in Snake's belly in seconds.

He dropped to all fours and frantically began to throw dirt out behind him. He glanced over his shoulder.

Snake was focusing on him. David's little clawed feet became blurs of motion. There was a steady plume of dirt standing up behind him, like a great brown bird feather.

Snake hissed. David saw its shadow arching, the great head readying to drop. The shadow moved forward.

David fell through to the tunnel with a clunk! Snake missed him by the breadth of a whisker. Scrambling to his feet, David scuttled blindly off down the passage, hoping against hope that Snake would not follow.

Nine

David ran until he was out of breath and had to stop. For a while all he could hear was his own gasping. But soon there was a sibilant cursing.

"Thisss one will get the far walker sssinger, yesss." The voice was far behind, but steadily approaching. "Thisss one can tassste it now."

With a start, David suddenly realized what Snake meant by 'taste.' It was that tongue. He could somehow taste the air the way Wolf and David sniffed it with their noses. He could find David even in this black tunnel! David had to run once more. As he set off he again regretted his lack of lemming sense underground. Any other of his clan would have had this maze figured out long ago. All David could do was keep moving and hope.

Opening after opening, passage after passage went by. He took forks, switchbacks and loops. Every time he thought that surely Snake must lose him. But each time he stopped to listen, the hissing was there. Sometimes far away, sometimes close, but always there.

David began to look for an escape passage. If he could get out first he would try the stream. Even a small chance was better than no chance at all!

He passed a series of openings that went down and to his left. He was sure that was away from the stream. He did not want to be caught in the open forest floor with Snake close behind. Now came a tunnel that forked off to the right. Praying it wasn't a dead end to a burrow, he scampered desperately along its dark course. Soon, it turned back to the left, then the floor tipped upwards. If it was a dead end, he would be surely trapped. There had been no side tunnels for a long time. He ran into the wall of dirt at full speed, nearly knocking himself unconscious.

"It hasss gone here, yesss." Snake had found his scent! "Thisss one got a fat mole in thisss hole before. It goesss nowhere."

David shook his head, trying to clear the stars from his eyes. He hit his head again when he did. It was a stupid tree root. A tree root! This must be an old escape passage, then. He began to dig. Almost immediately he popped out into broad daylight.

His heart soared when his eyes adjusted and he first saw the water. Then cold shock gripped his chest. He had not found the stream after all. It was the lake. He would never in the world be able to swim that vast expanse. Frantically he looked around, and instantly realized why that escape tunnel was no longer in use.

He was in an alcove. A tiny bay. The sides were straight up seamless rock cliffs, impossible to climb. Looking at the lake, he now noticed the lily pads. They looked large enough to support him easily, and went far out into the water. They even appeared to reach around the cove points. He might hop from one to the next if he had time. But Snake was close. Could he swim? David needed time. The tunnel must be blocked.

He rushed back to the opening and ripped at the walls until they collapsed. He only had time to do a quick job of it, so he knew Snake might soon work the opening clear. But he had a minute or two, and was glad for it. Quickly he returned to the water's edge and hopped out to the first pad. The force of even his small body landing there sent ripples out into the lake. He was about to jump to the second pad when he saw the faintest of movements below.

Perhaps it was because he had learned his lesson about caution earlier that day; or perhaps it was some ancient lesson handed down from his ancestors. No matter. Something made him hesitate. After staring for some seconds he was very glad he had. For there, almost invisible against the mottled bottom, and floating as if in midair, was a great savage fish. David had no doubt that had he advanced to the second pad it would have taken him for sure.

Now, he was truly trapped. With Snake behind, cliffs to either side and this thing in front, he had nowhere to go except to a choice of most uncomfortable ends. It was unendurable.

"Wolf!" he cried in anguish. "I am done!"

The fish moved. With no more than a casual flick of its fail, it drifted upwards and regarded him. Then it lifted its ferocious snout just out of the water and said: "Who are you that you know my other name?"

The question caught David totally off guard. There had been fish in the river by the field. He had seen them taking insects often. And as recently as his floating escape from Lynx he had seen trout. It had never occurred to him that they might talk.

"Your name?" he replied finally. "I don't know your name. I called out 'Wolf.' You are not one of his people."

The fish yawned. His cavernous mouth opened to reveal rows of teeth as thick and fearsome as a valley of thorns.

"I did not say my 'name,' for that is Pike. I said my 'other' name. Those who fear me, and that is everyone in this lake, also call me *waterwolf*. I was not aware that there was another kind. Pray tell me about this other 'Wolf.'"

David came close to losing his self-control then. Snake's hissing was growing louder with each passing second, there was no way out by land and this monster seemed interested in a little before-dinner conversation.

But David got hold of himself. An idea began to form in his quick brain. If Pike wanted something to eat, David might just be able to accommodate him after all. He bent forward and nibbled a chunk of the lily pad. It was bitter.

"My," he said, "this is the first time I have tasted this plant. It is very sweet." With a great effort, he swallowed the vile stuff. Then he said, "And have you eaten, sir?"

"Not today," said Pike, eyeing him closely.

"Well, then," said David, biting off another chunk of the terrible lily pad, "perhaps you would care to join me?"

"I do not eat such things."

"Of course," agreed David. "I was not suggesting that. I have other food nearby that I am sure would be more to your taste."

"And that is?"

"Snake."

The fish twitched. A feeling of elation poured through David. The other lemmings are right, he thought. I am quite mad!

"I will bring it to you," he said, turning as if to step to shore. Then he hesitated and looked back. Pike was beginning to quiver with anticipation. He did not take David's pause at all well.

"Well, get it! Get it!" he snapped impatiently.

"Yes," said David, nodding. "But I had forgotten. I must get across the lake, and I had planned on riding my snake. I do not swim great distances, you see."

Pike was shaking so that he looked ready to climb right out on shore in his eagerness. Yet he paused the briefest instant before he replied. When he did, there was the slightest edge of craftiness to his tone.

"That is no problem. I will take you across."

"On your back? I could not hold on. It is too round and smooth," said David. "But..."

"Yes? Yes?"

"Perhaps on a pad. You could push me, I suppose."

"That will be fine," growled Pike. "Now, the snake!"

"Certainly," said David, stepping to shore and walking back toward the blocked hole as though on a stroll. His calm was only for appearances. What he had in mind was desperately dangerous.

He began carefully to dig out the tunnel.

"Isss it the far walker sssinger? Yesss! It hasss come back! It knowsss we doesssn't mean it any harm, yesss!"

It was all David could do to keep digging. The horrible creature's excitement was growing. The hissing got louder and louder as the dirt began to give way. David pulled a bit more loose and, swallowing with a dry throat, stepped back several paces to wait.

Snake's writhing head was well out of the opening when David started singing the lullaby. It worked again. Snake's hissing ceased, its eyes grew cloudy and the tongue hung limp. David continued singing, but began to back up slowly toward the lake. Snake followed, as if in a dream. When they were two pads out from shore, David slid, shuddering, by the shiny black body and hopped to the bank. He stopped singing.

"There's your snake," he said to Pike. "Enjoy."

Snake never came fully from his dream. Pike exploded from the depths and took him in an explosion of water. There was a bit of thrashing about, but the contest had been decided the instant Pike sunk his teeth into Snake's body. The battle ended well below the surface, out of David's sight, to his relief. It left no more mark than some spreading rings and stray bubbles. In a few minutes, the water was again calm. A little while later, Pike appeared at the water's edge. There was a piece of bloody black skin hanging from his lower jaw. Caught on a tooth, it flapped like a flag of death when Pike spoke.

"I owe you a ride," he said, "do I not?"

David shuddered, but he said: "That was the bargain."

"When you are ready," said Pike.

David did not hesitate. He didn't dare for fear of losing his nerve. With absolutely no illusions about Pike's real intentions, he stepped out to the second pad and waited. Pike looked at him for a moment, as if considering something, then belched rudely and dropped below the surface.

David let out a stale batch of air from his lungs. So far, so good. He had been right in guessing that Pike would not try to eat him immediately after consuming something the bulk of Snake. But his manner had left no question in David's mind about his future plans.

The lily jiggled as Pike bit through the stem. It began to move slowly between the other pads. Soon, with Pike's snout pushing from behind, it entered open water and began to make for the far side. They were more than half way across when Pike said, "Can you see a large bay ahead?"

There was such a bay, the deepest notch of which ended at the foot of a great falls.

"Yes, I see it," said David. This must be it! The path to the high places! He must reach it. The answer was up there somewhere. He had to know. He had come too far not to!

"I live in that bay," said Pike. "Near the big log. Perhaps you can see that, too."

David said he did. It was obvious what he had hoped was true. Pushing from the rear of the big pad, Pike could not see where they were going.

"Kindly tell me when we are near my log so I can slow a little. The water is shallower farther on and I don't want to run aground."

"Certainly," agreed David. Now he knew Pike's plan! He intended on stranding David near the log and waiting until he had digested Snake before he had his lemming snack.

They passed Pike's log.

"We must be almost there," said Pike.

"Almost," lied David. He could see the bottom rising slowly toward him. They were well past the log when Pike said, "Are you sure you are looking at the right log? This seems over far."

"Is it the one with the old nest in the limbs?"

"That is the one."

"We've still some way to go," said David. "It probably seems farther because you are pushing the pad."

Pike said nothing, so David assumed that had satisfied him. He glanced at the bottom. Still too deep. If he went in now, he wouldn't have a chance. They began to enter the outflow from the falls. Then David saw the eddy. It was just like the one that had brought him to shore in the stream.

"I feel current," said Pike. "We must have passed my log."

"You have just eaten," said David, his voice cracking. "One tires easily after a meal."

"Just the same, I will look for myself, and — what?"

Pike's exclamation came after he had dropped back from the pad and realized where they were. The pad drifted to a stop at the edge of the eddy, but did not enter it.

David had no choice. He dove in, barely ahead of Pike. Just before he hit the water, he saw the pad disappear down a tunnel of teeth.

He bobbed to the surface. Pike was still down, gulping what he thought was a lemming in a lily pad. The swirling waters had David confused for a moment, then he got his bearings. With a few quick strokes, he pulled himself into the eddy and began to pick up speed towards shore. He reached for the beach with every bit of strength he had. He must find shallow water before Pike found him. A cry of rage split the air behind him.

He had been seen.

He dug in harder, tearing at the water as he would at a tunnel wall. The shriek came again, much closer. He felt a surge of water and looked back in horror.

The hideous jaws were spread wide. A roll of water preceded them...a great spiked wave of death that was almost on him. With the last of his strength he lunged ahead, lifting on the wave almost in Pike's mouth.

Then he was clear. The jaws snapped shut on empty air. Pike's full belly had run aground the length of a lemming's tail too soon.

David had been saved by Snake.

Ten

For a long time, David lay quietly on the sandy lakeshore. A soft evening settled over Pike's enraged cries. Slowly their force and shrillness abated. Still, David could see his wake, a silver "V" that ceaselessly worked back and forth not twenty feet away. With one last glance in Pike's direction, David got up and trotted toward the falls.

In a very short time he realized that from the far side of the lake he had failed to comprehend their actual size. They were enormous: a thundering, crashing sweep of descending water that sailed far out from the cliff top and fell slowly, majestically to the rocks far below. They were easily many times the height of the tall forest trees that stood right next to them.

The closer he got, the more awesome they became. The very ground trembled near them! It was hard to tear his eyes from such terrible beauty, but David did. The light was almost gone, and he wanted to see if he could decide on a path of ascent for morning. His studies did not reassure him at all. Finally, he gave it up and found a place to sleep.

The thundering and trembling ground were eerie bedfellows, but David managed snatches of sleep. When the sun arose in the morning, he was up with it. Because of the ever-present mist near the falls, there was sweet grass. David breakfasted and then made for the falls. In the full light of day, the way was clear. He dared not attempt the cliffs anywhere but near the falls. As far as he could see in both directions they were as bare of cover as his stone back at the field. Only next to the great cataract did anything grow.

The deed looked more and more unlikely with each passing minute. The only possible ascent was right next to the falls, up a nearly vertical cliff of mist-slimed stone with hardly a catch-hold. Lemmings are at home on rocky hillsides, and quite good at climbing, but David doubted any of his race had ever attempted anything half so ambitious as this. He sat down in the shadow of a boulder, leaned back against it and stared blankly upwards.

It was most fortunate he did, because at this moment a great bird sailed out over the falls, cupped its wings and descended with breathtaking speed to a tree. Just before it crashed into the uppermost branches, it flared and came to a perfect landing in the top.

Wolf had been right. David recognized Eagle instantly. Fortunately, the lemming had been quite close to the cliff. The beach was so small he had little choice about that. In the jumble of rocks and vegetation, one small creature shouldn't stand out. Still, when Eagle glanced momentarily in David's direction, he flinched. The thing was huge!

The fact that he had seen it cross the clifftop was amazing. At that distance, Hawk would seem the size of a gnat. But Eagle was clearly visible even to the outline of his cruel beak. No wonder Wolf had said this bird was to be feared above all hunters!

David had to remain perfectly still for a long while

until Eagle spotted something and sailed off across the lake. Scurrying as fast as he could, David barely found the cover of a root of a giant tree before the bird returned. It was scary the way he dipped below the lowest branches before catching an updraft and returning to the treetop.

If David hadn't known better, he might have feared he had been seen. Even so, he felt uncomfortable all that day, and stayed in his hiding place until well after dark. It gave him time to think, and more than once his mind drifted back to the field and Sheba. Was it worth it? Worth all the danger and hardship? He asked himself that question many times that long afternoon. The answer was always the same. It had to be.

With the evening, he began his climb. He had a plan for the first part of the way, at least. It was based on the fact that Eagle had arrived at the tree in the morning. If he preferred day hunting, then David should be safe after dark — at least until the moon rose. The first stretch would offer the additional protection of tree branches, as well. He felt fairly certain that if he didn't fall, or get swept from the cliff by the falls, he could at least manage the early climb in relative safety.

As it turned out, he was correct. The only danger he faced was the cliff, which was formidable. The rocks were so slick he had to make absolutely sure of every hold before he went for the next. It was a slow, tiring journey, but by the time the moon cleared the overhang he was in the uppermost cover. He found a crevice, wedged himself in it and fell into an exhausted and dreamless sleep.

He awoke cramped and hungry to find himself staring at Eagle's back. The sight of the great bird so close startled him. He had to stifle a cry of surprise.

Eagle was facing out toward the lake, obviously watching for prey. He apparently did not expect anything edible to appear on the bare cliff face. That was just fine with David, but he did not care to push his luck. He looked quickly around to see if there was any way to get some distance between the two of them.

The crevice was a possibility. It was veined with wrinkles, and might be climbed by bracing oneself across the gap. He glanced at Eagle momentarily. The bird had not moved. A part of David found the animal quietly magnificent. His head was strong, and as pure white as his tail. His wing feathers were longer than David's body. And those talons were twice as big as Pike's largest teeth. They looked strong enough to crush rock. Or lemmings. He began to work his way up the crevice.

The going was terribly slow. He had to jam his back feet against one side and walk upwards along the other with his front paws. Several times in the next hour, he found himself stretched almost to his claw tips. And ever with him was the fear that Eagle might become aware of him. There was no danger of being heard with the falls so close, but a single pebble dislodged and bouncing the wrong way could announce his presence as surely as if he had jumped on those powerful shoulders with all four feet.

Somehow he managed a good distance before the sun crested the cliffs. The crevice had widened and flattened out. David could no longer touch both walls, but it wasn't a problem. He was now in a steep, narrow gully and could climb easily. Best of all, it was now deep enough that he was well protected from prying eyes both below and above. His spirits lifted measurably until he realized where his path was leading. He was heading straight for the falls.

* * *

It was late afternoon. David stood in the crevice and stared at the wall of water before him. From far below came a rumbling, but here the sound was more of a hissing. It was as though all the snakes of the world had gathered in one place. David's problem was that he had to go in there.

When he had reached this spot a short time earlier, he had peeked out to see if he could locate a protected way up. What he had found was an overhang of featureless wet rock. An absolutely flat vertical face as gray as a rainy day. He didn't think a fly could hold on to that, and he *knew* he couldn't.

Below, it was much the same. Since he couldn't go up or down, and wouldn't go back, he had to go forward. That meant into the falls. He stepped beneath the torrent.

It was eerie. Tiny droplets of mist, as thick as blown dust, hovered about him. He was instantly soaked to the skin. The crevice floor was more slippery than before. To his right the water seemed caught in a moment of time. Though it was passing at very high speed, it appeared at the same time not to be moving at all. David wanted to be rid of this place. He hurried on.

In a matter of minutes he came to the end of the crevice. Now what? Was this the end of his journey? He felt a little mad, again. Maybe he should go back and demand that Eagle fly him to the top. Or perhaps swim up the falls?

The water streamers were very beautiful. Now, why had he thought they seemed to be standing still? There was a soft flowing to them, like lazy currents of wind through a grassy field. He could just step out and easily...

Suddenly he caught hold of himself. Must be tired, he thought. He shook his head to clear it. There was a way. He would have to find it. He hooked his front paws on the outer edge of the crevice and peered around in the mist. It was hard to see because his eyes kept filling with water. Between blinks he glimpsed another crack some way above. It would mean a long climb up the face of the slimy rock with the falls skimming inches away. For a moment, he hesitated.

He might be swept to his death. Should he go back down and look for another route? He didn't relish the thought. Besides, that was going back. He made up his mind. He would go on.

With a stubborn set to his jaw, he reached up and found a tiny indentation in the slick stone. Hanging by one paw, he felt around and found another, a little higher. He pulled himself up.

Paw over paw, he worked his way. An errant flume of water parted from the falls and nearly washed him away.

He held on. The climb seemed to take forever. The hissing, swirling world here stopped time. It was as though he had always been on this miserable, slimy stone face, drenched with numbing ice water and hanging on by a single claw.

He had to stop many times for rest. When he did, it was a fight to avoid staring at the falls. The odd patterns were beautiful, the bone-vibrating hiss strangely pleasant. It would be so easy just to let go and sail peacefully down with the lovely patterns, timeless, free forever....

He blinked. He was slipping! Frantically he scratched at the stone. He couldn't find a hold. He began to slide! Faster. Faster! He tore at the slimy face, shredding his claws.

And caught a crack.

For a long time he couldn't move — didn't dare move, because he was shaking so hard he almost dislodged himself. That had been close. Now, he understood something of what had happened to Snake. There are things in the world that can play tricks with the senses. Lullabies do it to snakes and waterfalls to far walkers.

Finally, he set off again, forced painfully to cover ground he had crossed before. But he wasn't caught by the trance again. He was too busy cursing his own carelessness to be distracted by anything so unimportant as a mere natural wonder.

When he reached the upper fissure, he found it large enough to be of use. He rested for a moment, then set off along it. His way was back toward the north, but he did not lose ground. The crack went up, widening as it crossed the face. In a short while he found himself free of the falls and within sight of the top.

He rested for a bit there, then peeked down over the ledge to see where Eagle was. It would be quite ridiculous to make it this far and then get picked off. He was nowhere to be seen. Still, David played it cautious, watching for a long time. The sun was dropping low in the west when he began the last ascent of the cliff.

It was stupid to make an easy climb in broad daylight, but he was sure Eagle was far away. And he was hungry. There might be sweet grass close by. He had not eaten for two days. He was within a few steps of the top, just below where the water sailed out into space, when the shadow appeared on the rock.

David's head jerked around. The setting sun was blinding. He turned away, searching for cover. The ledge he was on ran under the falls, but nowhere in the other direction. There was no niche, no boulder, no cover. And he had seen Eagle dive before. That meant there was also no time.

But he could see the shadow, he realized. That was as good as seeing the bird. By the way it was coming at him, right out of the sun, David guessed Eagle had probably known all along. He had been just waiting for the lemming to make a mistake, which was exactly what had happened.

David jerked his eyes toward the falls. He could run under them, but what would that solve? Eagle would just wait for another chance. If not today, then farther on, tomorrow.

Still, David hesitated. The shadow was growing.

There was a way. It was very, very risky.

"What isn't?" he asked himself, grimly.

The shadow grew. David's eyes narrowed and his chin jutted out. Eagle could not drop on him from above because of the cliff. He would have to come in straight and level, pulling up at the last moment to pick the lemming from his perch. It would be a tricky maneuver, but David didn't doubt Eagle's ability to do it. His only doubt was whether or not he could pull off a maneuver of his own.

He would know soon. Eagle was close. David, remembering Hawk, watched for the flaring of the wings. In spite of the direct warmth of the late afternoon sun, he found himself shivering. If he mistimed this one, he would soon be hanging from those talons. His legs were shaking. He forced them to be still.

Easy now, he thought. Take it easy. He's getting ready....

He saw the wings cup. He jumped for the falls, moving just slowly enough to give the impression he might still be catchable. Eagle swerved.

David's foot slipped into a crack. He was stuck! Frantically, he jerked his leg, trying to break loose. It was no use. The shadow grew, the wings flapping as the bird adjusted its flight, zeroing in on him.

Almost in a trance, David turned to look at his oncoming death. The claws were extended, coming at him like Pike's teeth.

Time suddenly seemed to slow to a crawl. The sound

of the falls disappeared, the feel of the cold spray. There was nothing but the great cruel beak, the fierce eyes, the flaring wings and those slowly approaching talons.

And then, it was over.

Eagle swerved at the last moment and flew right into the falls.

There was a horrible screech that mingled with the hiss of the water, then tapered off as the bird was swept toward the bottom. As quickly as he could, David worked his paw free, then slid back out in the clear and looked to the beach. There, just now bobbing from the swirling white froth, was Eagle. His wings were flapping uselessly against the current. For a moment, David thought he would be carried out into the lake to drown. But a lucky turn of current caught the bird and lodged it into the hollow of a boulder. Somehow, the battered giant managed to claw his way to the top of the rock, out of the torrent. His wings flapped feebly once more, then were still.

David watched for a moment longer. He felt a pang of sorrow for Eagle. He was, after all, one of the greatest of living things. Surely nothing else could have survived such a fall.

Then, it hit him. Eagle had turned away! At the last moment, he had turned away!

"Why?" he found himself saying out loud as he looked at the battered body far below. But there was no answer. Perhaps there never would be. He shook his head in confusion, looked once more at Eagle, then turned away and made for the top.

In a few minutes he crested the cliff and saw before him a clear way of stone. It followed the stream upwards, disappearing over a crest only to appear much smaller still higher up the mountain.

Many more times it disappeared and reappeared as David's eyes swept upwards until he saw the jagged white ridge that was the highest of all.

Jutting even above the clouds, the ridge stood forth, a ragged crest of stark rock and snow. Even from so far below, David could see the puffs of ice crystals being swept from the peak by the scouring winds. He shivered.

It was there he must go. It was there he might sing the last song that is the first song, the birth song that is the death song, and so perhaps find out who he was and why he lived.

He set off, a tiny figure taking tiny determined steps ever upwards. With every stride, he wondered again: would it happen to him, too? And, if it did, would he be able to stand what he learned?

Would he even understand the message?

Eleven

David's first night on the mountain was a miserable one. The barren ground was a cold jumble of rocks, twisted little pines and scabby patches of earth. No matter where he tried to hollow out a bed, he found stone. Finally, he curled up in the lee of a boulder. He couldn't sleep for shivering, so he gave up trying and just waited for a merciful dawn.

Dawn came, but it was far from merciful. A cold wind blew in from the west. By first light a drizzle began to soak the mountainside. It kept up throughout the day. Steadily, without good spirits, he climbed. By noon he had left all but the scraggliest pines behind. By late afternoon, even they were gone. Now, there was nothing but gray stone, pale lichen moss and the ever-present rain. Several times he tried feeding on the lichen. It was almost as bitter as the lily pad. He trudged on.

With the dawn of the second day, the weather cleared. He saw that he was on the fringe of the cloud mantle. He ate some of the lichen, then took a nap in the pale sunshine. Once, he awoke to see a great bird cross a patch of blue sky, then dip down toward the lake, far below. There was no mistaking the silhouette. Eagle was all right, after all. David felt good about that, and wondered again why the bird had spared him. He curled up against the stony ground and slept a little more.

It was late afternoon when he again set off. At least, it seemed to be about that time of day. The clouds had closed in around the mountain. But he wouldn't lose his way. All he had to do was keep heading up.

When even his good burrow eyes could make no way of it in the darkness any more, he lay down and drifted into fitful slumber. His dreams were all mixed up. Eagles with wolf jowls, snakes that had great talons, and flying pike. In spite of the high cold winds, he woke up once in a hot sweat. After that, the dream hovered close, enveloping him every time he began to slip away. Soon, he was afraid to sleep.

David lost track of the days. Traveling through that mist became a blur of lichen, darkness, cold, weariness and a path that would never end. Sometimes he caught himself wandering off the way. Once, he lost it for a very long time. But he just kept heading upwards, dropping when he could go no farther, then later staggering on.

He began to dream even as he walked. Visions of Sheba and the burrow floated serenely before him, calling him forward. Sometimes, Sheba was up ahead. There, by the singing stone! He would quicken his pace, but somehow never reach her. She kept calling, calling. David kept climbing, climbing.

Then one night he awoke to find himself standing in clear moonlight. Had it not been for the biting wind, he would have thought himself still dreaming, for the scene was unreal.

Everything about him was etched in silver. Jumbles of shimmering boulders littered the sides of luminescent vales like so many cold stars. The wrinkled ridge crests were pale, glowing spiderweb strands, glistening away in all directions. If it had been a web, he would have been in the middle. And that, he suddenly realized, meant he was at the top.

Now what? There was something he was supposed to do when he got here, but he couldn't remember what it was. He nibbled on some lichen. It tasted different from the plants he had found below. He slipped into a deep sleep with a final mouthful chewed but not swallowed.

He awoke to a full sun, and one of the most magnificent sights he would ever see. All around, the world fell away into a sea of clouds. Here and there, to the north and south, the tops of lesser mountains poked through the brilliant surface. Far to the west, the white glare broke up into little chunks that floated along like great, puffy islands.

Somewhere out there, he knew, was the field. And Sheba. Those lovely clouds were even now drifting over his stone, passing overhead as silently as they had on that first glorious day out of the burrow. The memory of the little lemming that he had been came to him as though it had sprung to life. He saw himself lying on his back on the stone, marveling at the clouds. It made him sad. He turned away to the east.

Here, the land fell away more slowly. There were fewer clouds. A short distance from the mountain, they disappeared into a soft haze that shimmered over a land of gold, brown and red. It was a vast, empty land. He could not see the end of it.

This was truly the highest of the high places. He could see why the far walker wolf had come here to die.

And why he might have learned many things that other wolves did not know. There was a feeling here. It was as if the stones themselves were aware; as if their silent vigil since the beginning of time had earned them a living spirit of their own.

He suddenly hoped there was knowledge here for him, too. Perhaps he would have to wait just like the stones. But he was weak. The air was thin, and did not nourish his lungs any more than the strange lichen seemed to feed his body. There was no water. He had to eat ice crystals for that.

In the end, though, there was no real decision to make. There was no place else in the whole land for him. He would find his answer here or not at all. So, he set to feeding on the lichen, and he set to thinking.

He had to sing a song.

The problem was, he didn't know which one.

In the days to come, he tried every song he knew. From the earliest lullaby, he sang them to the solemn mountaintop and pale sky. They vanished into the thin air like the dusty crystals of ice. He tried the laments of the dead and the outcast. These seemed to ooze downward and vanish into the misty canyons far below.

He tried summer songs, burrow songs, love songs, and sleep songs. Nothing seemed to work. He knew he was growing weaker by the day, but kept on.

Now, he turned to the songs he had learned from the other peoples. The song of the martin: sly, furtive, sinister melodies flitting through small, dark themes. The song of the hawk brotherhood: lofty spirals of pure tones ascending swiftly. He sang the killing song of the badger, the waking song of the lark, the evening song of the frog.

He tried the songs he had made up on his journey. He even tried the songs he and Wolf had sung on the hill.

And then there was nothing left. Not a song he had ever heard had he missed. Nothing had happened. The journey, all his narrow escapes, all his fear, all his triumphs — all for nothing.

He must not be a far walker, after all.

He felt terribly weary. The altitude and lack of rest and food had him near his limit. He should go back down, but where? He was outcast from his own kind and hunted by half the rest. Death waited him on a return trail, desolation lay to the east.

The thought came to him like the flight of a small bird.

It would be simple. He would just walk to the cliff. The same one where that ancient wolf, the real far walker, had probably stood. David got up and went toward the place. There was a small space free of boulders. He stopped for a while, thinking about things.

The drop was forever. He stared into the blue mists below, and was very calm. He should make up a song before he died. The problem was that he had covered everything one could sing about already. Maybe a song about singing, he suddenly thought. Yes. That sounded right. But it was hard to concentrate. The singing made it hard to concentrate.

Whoever it was, it didn't sound like Wolf. David wrinkled his nose. It was a strange song. High. Almost a keening, like the wind. He looked up from the precipice, and saw the clouds boiling toward the mountain. Like a vast, fluid night sky they rolled toward him. The folds were black as midnight. In them spears of lightning flickered. The mass surged over him with incredible speed, turning the day away with a great dark hand.

The song was wind. A storm of music. It was a tremendous thing, ripe with silent, roiling thunderheads, the crackle of brilliant spikes and a strange rich-smelling air.

Rain came. Rivers of rain. Great hissing waterfalls slanting backward from the racing clouds. The drops were half as large as David's head. When they swept across the crest, they seemed to wash the mountain of all but bare stone. But the waters separated when they came to David, and surged over the precipice, forming a cascading torrent many times the size of the great falls.

There were voices in the wind. He knew them. There was the clan chief lemming. "David is outcast!" And Hawk. "That mark is pride." And Wolf. "You are a far walker...a far walker...a far walker.... "

Wolf's voice subsided beneath the wind.

The raindrops splattered around him with the sound of lemming footsteps. The raindrops fed the torrents that were rushing past. Rivers of lemming-colored water sailed over the cliff, falling to crash into a blood-red sea.

* * *

David awoke. The sky was clear and dark. It was filled with stars, but not a trace of clouds. He felt a presence nearby, and turned his head. Standing there, his head as white as moonlit frost, was Eagle. It was as though David were not a part of the scene, but rather outside and observing it. He returned the great bird's fierce gaze with one of great calm. Eagle spoke:

"I have passed three times so close that my claws touched the fur of your head, yet you have not moved. Why do you not care about your death?"

"Does my caring about such things matter to you?" asked David.

Eagle's feathers ruffled as if from a breeze, though there was no wind. "Yes," he said, finally.

"Why did you not kill me at the falls?" asked David.

Eagle's head tilted. So much like Hawk, thought David. Though this one is greater, they are truly brothers.

"When you turned to look at me," said Eagle, "I saw the mark of the brotherhood on your forehead."

"Ah," said David, "that is one more I owe Hawk."

Eagle seemed unsettled. His feathers ruffled again. When he spoke, his voice was almost inaudible.

"Who are you?" he asked.

"My name is David," said the lemming.

Eagle paused again, his golden eyes searchingly on David.

"Then — *what* are you?" he asked.

"A far walker," replied David.

Eagle was silent for a very long time, yet his gaze never left David.

"There are legends of such things," he said, almost to himself. "There was a blind wolf long ago... "

His voice faltered. "Have — you seen something? Things others have not seen?"

"Yes," said David.

Eagle seemed moved. His eyes rested on David's mark. "How do you come to bear that?" he said.

David touched the mark. It seemed older than it was. As though it had been there before he was born. Perhaps, he thought, it had been.

"Does the mark of a brother need explanation?" he asked.

Eagle's beak worked soundlessly. His head tilted again.

"No," he said slowly. "It does not. A brother and a far walker. I do not understand. But I feel there is something I may do for you. Is there?"

The sound of the raindrops, the brown rivers cascading over the cliff and the sea of red, came back to David. He did not know exactly what it meant, but it left him with a great fear in his heart.

"Yes," he said quietly. "There is something you can do."

Twelve

In the high moonlight, Eagle and David soared westward. The great falls passed below. Pike's log passed by. David wondered if the old fish was still fuming about the loss of his meal. And there was the little cove where Snake had met his end.

The great forest began to slide beneath them. Lynx was down there somewhere, his great ears twitching as he stalked a rabbit in his dreams. Or a lemming.

"You might even find some of what you seek along the way," Wolf had said. "Some of my journeys have taught me more than what I found at the end."

What had he learned? That great cats despise water? That snakes slept when one sung them a lullaby? That you could outwit a pike? Surely, all of these. Yet, there was something more. It was like the songs. He had tried every song he knew up on that mountain and nothing had worked. Yet, somehow, out of all his songs had come the one song. Wolf had been right. If one journeyed well, destinations would take care of themselves.

But Wolf had said something else.

He had said, "There is a danger in such questions."

The forest was coming to an end. Behind, the sun was beginning to rise over the eastern horizon. They flew on in silence, crossing the scrubland and finally approaching the field.

"It seems so peaceful," he said.

"These heights have a way of creating that illusion," said Eagle.

"We will have to land," said David.

They began to drop. The wind whistled past David's ears. Tears formed in his eyes. He refused to close them. The field was empty. Not a feeding lemming in sight.

Eagle flared his wings and landed atop David's stone. It was too quiet. David hopped off Eagle's shoulders and sped down the field toward Sheba's burrow. He stopped at the entrance and listened. There should have been the rustlings of waking lemmings. There should have been the easy morning chatterings and happy laughter that typified his kind.

There was only silence.

With a lump forming in his throat, David scurried down the passage. The burrow was empty. He searched every nook and cranny, even the little niche behind the root where he had first seen Sheba. The place was cold and lifeless. Nobody had slept here in a long time.

He ran out the escape passage and rushed down into his family's burrow. It was empty, too. As though mad, he ran from burrow to burrow, searching, calling. There was no sign of life anywhere. Finally, emerging from the last tunnel completely out of breath, he collapsed on a clump of dead grass.

Everyone was gone.

The tears in his eyes were not caused by the wind this time. What had happened? Why had a clan that had been so long in one place suddenly disappeared? What could cause a burrow-loving race to leave home and safety like some mad far walker?

Eagle lifted from the hill and landed nearby.

"They are not here?" he asked.

David shook his head.

"I can understand why."

David looked at him sharply.

Eagle shrugged. "The reason is clear. You're sitting on it."

David got up. What was the bird talking about? He

looked at the patch of grass for a long time before he began to understand.

It was dead. The grass was dead. He ran to the river. What had been a deep flow was a trickle in the middle of a cracked dry mud flat. Even the willows, once rich and green, were dead. He ran back to the hill and clambered up on the stone at the top. What he saw astonished him.

Why had he not been aware of it from above? Had it been the long morning shadows? The wind tears? His false hopes?

It didn't matter. He hadn't seen it; not from above or in the vision or in his worst nightmares had he ever seen anything like the scene that surrounded him. But then he remembered. At the top of the great mountain, looking east, he had seen something like this: a desolation that stretched forever. A land wearing a brittle coat of death.

Now he knew why they had left. It was leave or starve.

But which way had they gone? Just like all the rest of the times in his life, it seemed the answer to one question only created another question.

Eagle walked up the hill, an awkward-looking bundle of feathers while on the ground.

"There are no tracks that I can see, far walker."

"The wind has them, I suppose," said David.

"Then we will follow the wind," said Eagle.

Thirteen

"Tell me again of your vision, far walker."

They were circling in a column of rising air, high above the field. With each turn, David's eyes could see farther, but there wasn't a living thing anywhere.

"What could have caused such a thing?" said David.

"Such dry times are common east of the mountains," said Eagle. "And I have seen something like this hereabouts before, though it was not so severe. Tell me again of your vision. It may give us help."

"I don't see how," said David. But he again related the tale of the storm, the raindrops, the river that parted around him and fell from the cliff.

"You say it was a brown river, but it fell into a red sea. Did you recognize the sea?"

"I have never before seen one," said David. "All I know of seas is what Wolf has told me. And none he described are red."

"Nor," said Eagle, "are any I have seen. There is a great one to the west, but it is blue. I have heard of one far to the east, beyond the wide plains. I do not know its color."

"Wolf has traveled all of the north," said David. "The seas there are all frozen."

"Then the red sea must be to the south. We will see if we can find it."

Eagle beat his great wings twice, and with David clutching to the feathers between his shoulders, left the thermal updraft and soared south. They flew all that day without stopping. The farther they went, the worse the desolation became. The riverbeds didn't even support trickles any longer, and the fields were nothing but bare earth. Clouds of dust the size of mountains flowed silently along on the dry winds. David didn't believe anything that walked could live inside them.

They rested that night on a baked and burnt cliff. Neither had anything to eat. In the morning they flew on.

Eagle was an expert at riding the great updrafts that lifted from the scorched earth, but even a sparrow could have soared in the rising blasts from this baked wasteland. Midday passed without a sight of a living thing. Evening was approaching when a glint that David could not see caught Eagle's sharp eyes.

"There is water ahead," he said.

Both hope and fear were kindled in David's heart. He didn't see how any lemming, even he, could have traveled on foot through what he had just flown over. The sun was down, but still giving light, when they began to descend toward the water.

"This is bad," said Eagle.

At first, David could not make out what was happening below. His eyes were no match for Eagle's. Then gradually, to his horror, he began to make sense of it, if there could be any sense to what he saw.

At the center of what had been a lake many times the size of the great water at the foot of the falls, was a pool no larger than the field. On the sloped approaches to this pool lay the remains of countless animals. At the edge of the water a great battle was being fought. Cats, bears, coyotes, rabbits, snakes, birds, deer and crawling things David had no name for were tearing at each other to get at the water.

As David watched, a rabbit attacked a coyote with such ferocity that the larger animal actually gave ground. Then the rabbit charged on a great cat with such a piercing scream that for a moment it looked as if even this one would step aside. But it didn't, and with a swipe of its claws the rabbit was ribbons of bloody shreds floating on the water, its life fluid sending a red stain spreading into the pool.

It reminded him of his vision. But this was a pool, not a sea, and there were no lemmings to be seen. He almost wished there were. It would mean his ordeal was over; that he would finally know, one way or the other.

Eagle swooped close, picking up some of the water in his beak. Some droplets splashed back to land in front of David. As thirsty as he was, he could not bear the thought of drinking. In a moment, they were reaching for the heights again. They flew in silence for a long time. Finally, it was David who spoke:

"If you wish, you can leave me somewhere and go back to feed."

"I am hungry," said Eagle. "But I could not add to the misery of those creatures. There are some things more important than food. One is living with yourself."

That night they slept on a high mountain. The next morning they awoke to see the southern sea. It was blue.

* * *

All the next day, while Eagle hunted, David sat on the pinnacle and hated that sea. It seemed to get bluer with each hour, as if intentionally taunting him. He sank into a deep depression, and didn't even notice the afternoon waning, or Eagle returning.

"Far walker?"

David came out of his trance.

"Yes?"

"I said I have brought food, and news," said Eagle. In one of his talons he had a handful of beach grass. He dropped it in front of David, but the lemming pushed it away.

"You must eat, far walker," Eagle said gently.

"Why?" said David. "It doesn't matter any more. The world is ending. Your eyes are better by far than mine, and even I can see that!"

Eagle pushed the grass back toward David. "What you say about the world ending may be true, but what you say about seeing far is not. My eyes can pick out a field mouse from a mountaintop. Your eyes can see tomorrow. There are deeds yet to be done."

"To what purpose?"

"That will be given to you, far walker, not to me. My part is to give aid: to use what abilities I have to help you. I have done that today. I have news."

"I am not interested. Go away."

Eagle went on as if he had not heard David: "During my hunt I found a great emptiness in the sky around me. My shore brothers were gone. This was strange, because there is food in these waters. Then I met an old jaeger. He told me the others had gone to the north to see a wonder that was happening there. A great migration. When I asked him what animals were in this migration, he said he did not know, but that it was said they were as an endless river on the land. Perhaps that is the river in your vision, far walker."

David looked at Eagle wearily. "Why should you think so?"

"He said that the animals were brown, and so was the river."

Fourteen

It was morning, but David felt it was afternoon. He was tired of far walking and visions and searching. David was tired to the bone of going without food or sleep, of facing danger, of searching for the meaning of meaningless dreams. And he was tired of staring into the face of death. He was so tired of that, he felt he would almost welcome his own death just to be finished with all the pain.

Eagle flew north along the coast. The winds were southerly so their progress was swift. But the hours glided by like the land below, silent and bleak. It was very late in the afternoon when Eagle dipped slightly.

"There," he said. "Do you see it?"

David roused himself, fighting back the weariness. He tried to shade his eyes with a paw. The red glare of the sun, the deeply shadowed land, made viewing difficult.

"The birds," said Eagle.

There was a soft blur. Gradually it became a cloud that seemed to be moving of its own will. Eagle dropped toward this strange thing. Now David could see that it was a great mass of individual birds wheeling and diving over something near the sea. Finally, he saw what that something was: the great brown river of his vision.

Lemmings without number. More than the stars in the sky. More even than all the stones in all the streams. And, as in his vision, the great river was flowing over the cliff and into a sea that was red. Red with the setting sun, and red with their blood.

"Sheba!" he cried. "Sheba!"

It was fruitless. His voice was drowned out in the maelstrom of sound that surrounded the dying lemmings. David had thought the battle of the desert pool had been terrible. It was nothing to this. As the lemmings approached the sea their flow was narrowed by a gauntlet of hunters. Foxes, ferrets, badgers, mink, martens and wolves ravaged them. From above came jaegers, owls, hawks and ospreys. The air was torn with the terrible barking, howling, hissing, shrieking and crying. It was foul with the stench of death.

Those who survived that gauntlet came to the high cliff. The crush of lemmings behind forced them over the edge, and the rocks far below were littered with uncountable broken bodies. Somehow, some did not die on the rocks, but hit the surging water. David knew how well lemmings could swim.

Even as he looked, a soft-furred girl lemming slipped below the surface. Then a form many times larger than Pike slid silently toward her sinking, twisting form. David averted his eyes. He realized he was crying.

"Sheba... " he said softly.

"David!"

His head jerked around. He knew that voice! But, how could he find even that great one in all this? Then came the song he knew so well. It guided his eyes to Wolf, who was standing near the edge of the cliff.

"Down there!" David told Eagle.

"Have you seen her?" cried David after they had landed. "Have you seen Sheba?"

"There are too many, David," said Wolf. "How could you find just one among them?"

David dove into the fringe of the lemmings. "Sheba! Sheba! Where are you?"

He was carried along toward the cliff. He fought his way back to Wolf.

"Wolf! Eagle! She can't hear me. Stop the hunters! Stop the noise!"

Wolf leapt foward, savagely attacking a group of nearby hunters, including some of his own people. Eagle leapt into the air and turned his beak and talons against the brothers. A jaeger fell from the sky. A wolf dropped to the ground, his throat torn from his neck.

David charged into the flow. It was thinning a little. The land hunters were backing away from Wolf's ferocity. But the brothers still dived and killed.

A terrible shriek came from above. David looked up to see an owl explode in a cloud of feathers. But it wasn't Eagle who had hit him!

"We meet again!" called Hawk. "And now you are a far walker. Truly you have worn your mark well!"

"She can't hear me!" cried David.

"We will stop them, far walker!" called Hawk, beating his wings and lifting quickly toward a group of diving gulls.

David was being pushed toward the edge. He bit and clawed his way through the slack-faced animals. Sheba was not anywhere to be seen. Fear for her raged in his heart. Had she already gone over the edge? Had she been taken by one of the hunters? Was his terrible journey for nothing?

A pure white-hot anger exploded in David's breast. Like a hunter he lunged at the approaching lemmings, his claws and teeth slashing at every lemming around him. The tide parted as if on command, leaving the two brown rivers of his vision flowing around him and over the precipice.

Then it was suddenly silent. The hunters had withdrawn.

From far below came the soft thunder of crashing waves and the pitiful mewling of dying lemmings. But around David was the patter of a multitude of lemming feet. It was the sound of raindrops. His vision was complete.

"David!"

"Sheba!" he cried. "Where are you?"

"Here, David! Over here!"

Then he saw her. She was with the last of them. Her once-beautiful coat was ragged and dirty. She was being carried along by those around her; too weak, obviously, to resist. David leapt forward, terrified. Could he reach her in time?

Blindly, the lemming river flowed toward the cliff. David ripped at those about him. He bit anything that came near, knocking over those who would not give way.

Sheba was nearing the edge.

David's fear for her exploded once more into rage. He slashed at the dumb beasts in his way, literally throwing them aside in one final desperate lunge for Sheba. Expending his last reserves of strength, he caught her at the very brink.

They teetered. The bloody waves crashed below them. The world was frozen. Time had stopped.

David had not eaten in days, nor had he slept. His fear and anguish had drained his soul. Even these last of the lemmings seemed without number. He realized he did not have the strength to fight free.

"I knew you would come," said Sheba. "I never gave up hope."

"I have come too late," said David, feeling his weariness to the marrow of his bones. The press of bodies would sweep them over in an instant. "I am sorry."

A lemming stumbled into him. He began to fall, but Sheba caught him and somehow pulled him back. Then she staggered between David and the oncoming bodies.

The sight of the battered, dirty, brave Sheba standing as a shield touched his soul. Like a torn, bloody battle flag, his own courage fluttered back. He got to his feet and moved to her side. The bodies came at them. Together, they pushed and bit and clawed — not to make headway, but to hold their ground.

Time began to move again, but flowed like the sap of a tree. Each instant oozed by, an eternity of scratching and biting and shoving just to hold that one tiny piece of earth. It came, finally, that he could no longer even find the strength to take in breath. The world began to spin. His paws dropped to his sides. He turned to Sheba to say goodbye.

But it was over.

The last of their kind tottered by, following the herd to their deaths. David and Sheba were alone on the cliff. They stared silently at the carnage below.

"It was the grass, wasn't it?" he said after a while.

She nodded. "There was nothing to eat. We had to leave our burrows. We just began to walk. Then the others joined us. I don't know how it could come to this."

"It was the madness," said David. "It wasn't me, after all. They had it in them all the time."

There was the sound of padding feet, and of wings. Wolf trotted up to them. Eagle and Hawk landed nearby. Then all the hunters came. All the foxes and ferrets and badgers and mink and martens and jaegers and cats. They formed a semicircle around David and Sheba. She trembled, but David said: "It's all right. The best of these are my friends."

Fifteen

David and Wolf watched the little lemmings playing beneath the September moon. After song, the two friends had argued easily about which of the youngsters would turn out most like David. Sheba had come out of the burrow and called the children inside. After that, the hill and the field lay quiet.

In silent agreement, David and Wolf sat watching. Soon, a small head popped out of the burrow entrance and slipped quietly away toward the river. It was Peter. Wolf had won the bet.

"You always were a good judge of character," said David.

"You haven't done badly," said Wolf.

David could not argue that, on the whole. With the recent rains, the sweet grass had come. There was more than enough now for his small family. Also, with the sudden scarcity of lemmings hereabouts, there was a similar lack of hunters. David's offspring would have little to fear during their lives.

And there was Sheba. Beautiful Sheba.

Not a better wife and mother existed among any of the peoples from the mountains to the sea. He was a lucky lemming, indeed.

"Now, what's this about a new song?" asked Wolf.

"Oh," said David, "it's nothing, really. Just a little verse I thought sort of summed things up."

Wolf laughed. "Well, let's hear it. It can't be any worse than listening to your false humility!"

David looked at the fields and the mountains. He sang:

Far I've wandered, far I've roamed
On strange pathways all alone.
Storm and wind have hearkened near
Around my head their tales to tell
About the way things soon will be
Upon the seasons of time's tree

Darkest burrows run beyond
Trails we know, and past the sun.
Races caring not for youth,
Love or beauty, or for truth,
In misty dells dwell evilly
Where from them even light will flee.

They stand as stone, both cold and dead,
As if to bring their horrid dread
To one and all — but always fail!
Because one comes with right and will,
And with the aid of one yet more
Whose mark he left upon his fore.

The journey's long and hard and bad,
And much that happens will be sad.
But still the seasons always turn,
And on time's tree spring flowers burn.
And wanderers no more alone
Are burrow bound — far walker's home!

Finished, David looked at Wolf. Wolf smiled that astonishing smile of his.

"So, far walker, it is as simple as that, eh?"

David blushed. "I don't understand what you mean."

Wolf grew thoughtful. For a short while he did not even look at David, his gaze remaining fixed on the far eastern mountains. Finally, he did speak.

"That is a question you will have to answer. You are the far walker, not me. But, I will try. It seems to me that your song is full of answers, yet you and your family are alive today because you were full of questions. So, if there is any truth in your journey it is that."

David nodded. "I think I understand," he said. "You mean that what happened to the rest of my clan came as a result of too much acceptance of things as they were. Believing that nothing would or even should change."

Now it was Wolf's turn to nod in agreement. "That is very much what I meant, David. It is a true thing even among my people, wanderers that they are, that custom is comfortable, more so than seeing things in a new way. The world keeps its own counsel. It changes as it will. Those who would see things as they were rather than as they are cannot hope to survive long."

David smiled. A bright look flashed across his face.

"So, my friend," he said, "you are saying that the adventure is not over?"

Wolf looked at David quietly.

"For you, for now, perhaps it is. What may come later, I cannot say." Once again, the great muzzle swung to the east. It came to David suddenly. Wolf would have to leave.

"You must return to your pack, of course," he said. "How stupid of me. But you'll be back soon?"

"I do not think so. The dry time has killed much more than lemmings."

David wrinkled his nose. He hadn't seen a rabbit around for a long while, come to think of it.

"Well, then, where will you go?"

"Across the mountains," said Wolf. "There are still some trails I have not walked, far to the east. I have heard of a great river beyond the plains. Game should be plentiful there."

"Yes," said David. "Sounds interesting. I should like to see those places. Perhaps we can go together some time. When things are in hand hereabouts, of course."

Wolf was silent for a moment. "I would like to share that journey with you, David. But for now we have different paths to walk. It may even be that we shall not see each other again in this world. But as surely as there are seasons on your tree of time, there will be another David and another Wolf. We will be as much a part of them as the ancient far walkers were a part of us, I think."

He stood up, stretched and walked to the rim of the hill. David's throat was suddenly thick. He had seen the eastern lands from the mountain top. They had no end. He truly might be looking at Wolf for the last time.

"Fare well, far walker," said Wolf, quietly slipping over the rim of the hill. "May the spoor be fresh!"

"And your kill swift," David called after him. "Fare well, old friend!"

Moments later, Wolf appeared far out in the field. He turned and sang out one long note. Then he was a shadow among shadows.

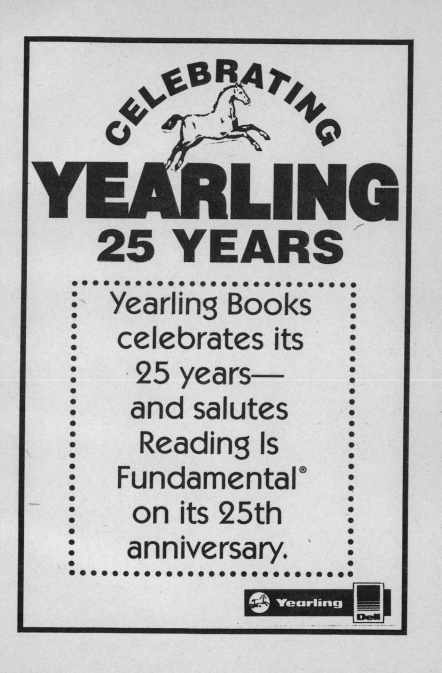